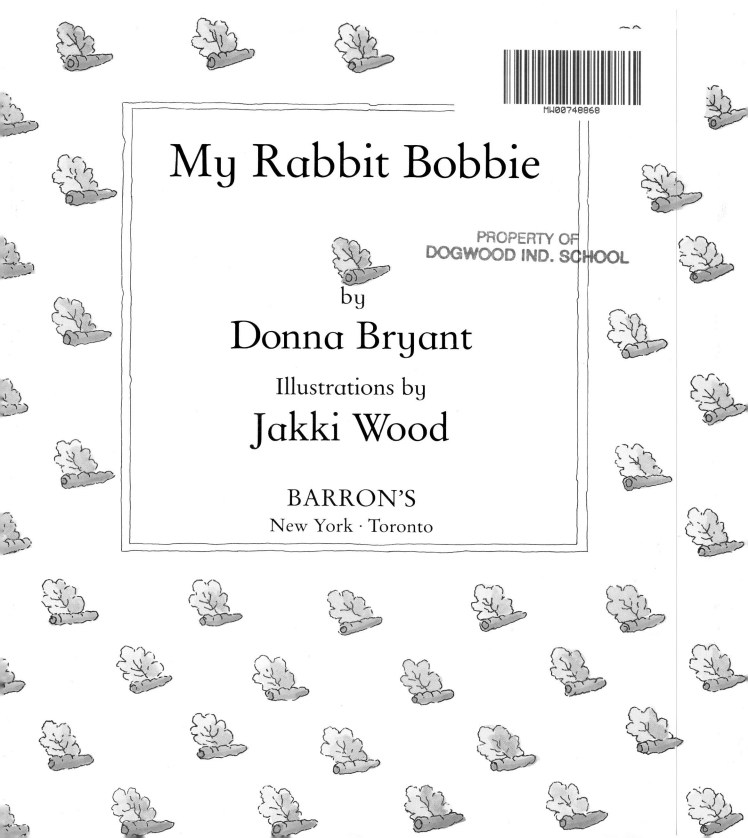

My Rabbit Bobbie

by

Donna Bryant

Illustrations by

Jakki Wood

BARRON'S

New York · Toronto

Every morning I go outside

to feed my rabbit, Bobbie.

She loves rabbit food and
wholewheat bread.

She has carrots and apples for a treat.

While I change her water bottle...

Bobbie plays in her clean straw.

Then she washes herself.

She is very good at washing her ears.

Bobbie has long back legs for hopping
and jumping,

and strong front legs for digging.

She gets along well with my friend's guinea pig,

and she likes to tease our cat!

When it's cold, Bobbie plays inside
with me.

Sometimes she's naughty!

Bobbie loves to be stroked and brushed,

and when she yawns I can see her
big teeth.

Bobbie is part of our family.

I love my rabbit.

First edition for the United States, Canada, and the Philippines
published 1991 by Barron's Educational Series, Inc.

Text © Copyright 1991 by Donna Bryant
Illustrations © Copyright 1991 by Jakki Wood

My Rabbit Bobbie was conceived, edited, and produced by
Frances Lincoln Ltd, Apollo Works, 5 Charlton Kings Road,
London NW5 2SB

All inquiries should be addressed to:
Barron's Educational Series, Inc.
250 Wireless Boulevard
Hauppauge, New York 11788

International Standard Book No. 0-8120-6210-8
Library of Congress Catalog Card No. 90-47924

Library of Congress Cataloging-in-Publication Data
Bryant, Donna.
  My rabbit Bobbie / by Donna Bryant : Illustrations by Jakki Wood.
    p. cm.
  Summary: A girl describes how she feeds, plays with, and loves her
pet rabbit Bobbie.
  ISBN 0-8120-6210-8
  [1. Rabbits as pets–Fiction.] I. Wood, Jakki, ill. II. Title.
PZ7.B837Myb 1991
(E)–dc20   90-47924
                                                  CIP
                                                  AC

PRINTED IN HONG KONG
1234 0987654321